Pocahontas

Illustrated by Meryl Henderson

Pocahontas

Leslie Gourse

ALADDIN PAPERBACKS

First Aladdin Paperbacks edition August 1996
Text copyright © 1996 by Leslie Gourse
Illustrations copyright © 1996 by Meryl Henderson

Aladdin Paperbacks
An imprint of Simon & Schuster
Children's Publishing Division
1230 Avenue of the Americas
New York, NY 10022

Printed and bound in the United States of America

12 14 16 18 20 19 17 15 13 11

Library of Congress Cataloging-in-Publication Data
Gourse, Leslie.
Pocahontas / Leslie Gourse. — 1st Aladdin pbk. ed.
p.   cm. — (Childhood of famous Americans)
Summary: Examines the life of the Indian princess Pocahontas
and her contact with English settlers, especially John Smith.
ISBN-13: 978-0-689-80808-1
ISBN-10: 0-689-80808-9
1. Pocahontas, d. 1617—Juvenile literature. 2. Powhatan Indians—
Biography—Juvenile literature. 3. Jamestown (Va.)—History—Juvenile
literature. [1. Pocahontas, d. 1617. 2. Powhatan Indians—Biography. 3.
Indians of North America—Biography. 4. Women—Biography. 5. Smith,
John, 1580-1631. 6. Jamestown (Va.)—History.] I. Title. II. Series:
Childhood of famous Americans series
E99.P85P5735   1996
975.5'01'092—dc20
96-1522
[B]

For Maria Franco George

Illustrations

Numerous smaller illustrations

Contents

Pocahontas

A Feast Is Planned

TWELVE-YEAR-OLD POCAHONTAS, a princess of the Powhatan tribe, awoke with a start. There was an unusual amount of noise in the longhouse of her father, Chief Powhatan.

The women of the royal family were arguing about how much deer, raccoon, oyster, fish, squash, pumpkin, and corn they should prepare. There was going to be a feast tonight.

Nobody knew exactly how much wood they would need to keep the fire going under all the clay cooking pots, either.

Little children lined up to bring the food

from the hut where it was stored. This long-house stood by itself a distance from the village. Chief Powhatan's guards protected it all the time, because it held all his royal treasures along with the food.

Women were grinding corn with their wooden mortars and pestles to make into cornmeal cakes. Usually only a few women prepared the corn for the daily meals of the Powhatan Indians, but today many of them were working at the task.

"What's going on?" Pocahontas asked the youngest wife of her father. The young woman was using a fine brush of reeds to paint pictures of flowers on the calves of her legs. She had mixed a red powder with walnut oil to color her shoulders and face.

"It's very exciting," she replied. "We're going to have a feast tonight. Your uncle, Chief Opechancanough, has sent messengers. He is bringing an Englishman to the longhouse. They found the man in the woods a couple of weeks ago.

"He was looking for food. He had gone far away from the English village on the Powhatan River." (The English called it the James River.) "He had taken his canoe along the Chickahominy River" (which the English called the York) "until the river became too narrow. Then he got out to walk on the land. Our people didn't know who the Englishman was or what he was doing on Powhatan land."

Another of Powhatan's wives was listening to Pocahontas and Powhatan's youngest wife.

"How do you know this?" the second wife asked.

"I heard the messenger's tale when he arrived at dawn. I was having berries and corn bread with Powhatan. The berries are very sweet this year."

"Yes, they're especially good," the other wife said. "Can I use some of your paint? I want to decorate my legs, shoulders, and face, too. But I have run out of red paint."

"Oh, tell me more about the Englishman!" Pocahontas said. "This is very exciting. I have been visiting the village of the English all summer. My father keeps sending me there with corn and deer meat, because the English don't have enough to eat. I wonder which Englishman is coming?"

"I don't know," the youngest wife said. "You are allowed to visit the English, but I have never even seen a white person."

The second wife dipped her brush in the paint. "Your father will have to decide what to do with these people who have come to live near us. Only your father, the chief of us all, can decide. Your father's will is law. And all the other chiefs trust his judgment."

"Where is my father?" Pocahontas asked.

"I believe he's in his private room." Her father's youngest wife painted a pinecone on her ankle.

Both women wore traditional doeskin skirts trimmed with beads at the waist and fringes at the hem. All the Powhatans, men and women, wore the same type of skirt. Each one of them liked to paint colorful designs on their bodies. They wanted to look different from one another and create their own styles.

All of them painted their upper bodies and heads with red paint. It helped them ward off the cold in winter. In summer, the paint stopped the mosquitoes from biting.

Around their necks they wore beads sculpted out of shells and pearls scraped from the insides of oyster shells.

The Indians also crafted their own leather

bags and decorated them with beads. They carried tobacco in the bags.

Pocahontas was too young to decorate herself in all these ways. But she did wear beads around her neck, and for special occasions she put feathers in her hair.

Now, her bright dark eyes searched the longhouse. She didn't see her father anywhere in the public places.

The youngest wife said to Pocahontas, "Why don't you look for your father in his private room? You are allowed to go there."

Pocahontas went to see if Powhatan was sitting by himself. He was the chief, or *werowance*, of his own tribe, the Powhatans, and he was also the emperor, or *mamana-towick*, of about thirty tribes in about two hundred villages of all sizes. All of them spoke the Algonquian language.

This village, where Pocahontas lived, was

called Werowocomoco.

All the tribes paid tributes to Powhatan. In return he pledged to help protect them.

Many times he stayed alone to think about his responsibilities and make plans. Pocahontas found him in his special place. It was blocked off by walls of birch bark at one end of the longhouse.

Pulling aside a curtain of reeds, she peeked in and saw him. He was sitting on his mat, also made of reeds, eating walnuts, hickory nuts, and chestnuts from a clay bowl placed next to him.

He was wearing his doeskin skirt tied at his waist. His shiny, sumptuous fur cape made from many raccoon skins was hanging from a peg on the wall. On the floor near his mat was his bed of tree branches covered with animal skins. He had set out a collection of white feathers on the floor. He was going to

17

wear them in his hair for the feast.

"May I come in, Father?" Pocahontas asked.

"Yes, come in, Matoaka," he said, calling her by her clan name. She had been called that at birth. Afterward she had been nicknamed Pocahontas.

The Powhatans believed everyone should have two names. One should be spoken but the other was to be kept a secret. Pocahontas was her spoken name. Both names meant "mischievous."

"I have been thinking about you," Powhatan said. "Do you know what is going on?"

Pocahontas sat down in front of her father. "They say that Uncle Opechancanough is bringing an Englishman here for a feast."

"That's right," Powhatan said.

"Is he an Englishman from the village where I deliver food?"

"Yes. That is the only English village here," Powhatan said.

Pocahontas looked seriously at her father. "You never went there yourself. But you saw English people before in the north country beyond the great lakes, didn't you?"

"No, I was never there myself. I told you that. Don't you remember?"

Pocahontas smiled. "Well, I love to hear you tell stories about the old days."

"I never saw Englishmen in the north country. My father's father came from the north. There our people hunted moose and buffalo. But the weather was very hard. Winters were long and cold. We wanted an easier life.

"So my father's father led our people down from the north country. They found this good land with saltwater rivers and sweet, freshwater rivers filled with fish, mussels, and oysters. The forests were crowded with wonderful animals. We hunted squirrels, deer, beavers, rabbits, raccoons, opossums, and turkeys. Some walked right into our village. They begged us to catch them. *Ha ha!*

"The ground was rich for planting corn, beans, and squash. We found blueberries for food, and gourds so we could make instruments for our dances, and walnuts good for eating and mashing into a milky drink. My father's father wanted to stay here. I was born here. And that is why you are here.

"You are just like our fathers. You have the courage to explore," Powhatan continued. His rare smile lit up his dark eyes.

"I wonder if I could ever be the chief of our people," Pocahontas said thoughtfully. "What an honor that would be! I would be called a *werosqua*, just as a man is called a *werowance*."

21

"Maybe some day."

"But how will I ever know enough?" Pocahontas asked. "I suppose it doesn't matter. You will live forever."

"Not forever, little one," her father said. "Neither you nor I will live forever. But you are my treasure, and one day, you will become a wife, and you will have a child who is your treasure, too. And perhaps you will even be a *werosqua*."

Pocahontas jumped up and turned a cartwheel across her father's private room.

Powhatan became serious again. "If you want to turn cartwheels, go outside and play with the children. I must think about the Englishman. My brother has told me the Englishman has a magic toy. It's a little round toy with tiny arrows inside it. My brother is afraid of it, but I know those tiny arrows can't hurt anyone. Why does my brother worry about toy arrows? Sometimes I wonder how I can have such a silly brother.

"I think the English want to stay here," Powhatan said. "We may have to fight to protect our land. There is no way we could win if they thought we had only bows and arrows. They have guns with bullets. I will continue to give them food if they will trade some of their guns in exchange for the food. I want their beads, too, of course, and their metal pots and tools. My people can use them. What do you think of that, my little mischievous one?"

Pocahontas crouched down and rested her chin on her hands. "They should give you what you want in exchange for food. They would starve without you. But maybe you will never have to struggle with the English. Maybe they can just stay in their own village, and we can live as we always do."

"That is a nice thought, Pocahontas," Powhatan said.

"You never saw an Englishman in the north country? So have you ever seen an Englishman before?" she asked.

"Yes. A group of English people came to settle on my lands when you were still a baby. They said they were planning to stay a short time. But I saw that the men and women were building houses. Our people went to war with them. The English lost that war. Many of them were killed. The rest of them left."

"I'm happy you won that war. But it's terrible that the English should die."

"They should have stayed in their home village. But they came in boats with sails, just as this new group of English people have done. They came from very far across the waters. Our canoes cannot go that far. But we have no need. We have everything we need right here for ourselves, for our children and our children's children." Powhatan stared into space and chewed a chestnut slowly. "We have everything we need."

Pocahontas picked up a shiny brown wild turkey feather and put it in her own hair. "May I wear this today?"

"Yes. But you should also wear your white feathers, because they signify peace. Let's take a walk around the village, little one. I want to see to the preparations for tonight."

A Special Guest

POWHATAN PICKED up a jar of oil and rubbed it on Pocahontas's shoulders to protect her from the chilly air outside. He rubbed oil on his own chest.

It was a sunny day. The air wasn't cold enough for him to put on his long fur robe. Pocahontas didn't need her little beaver cape, either.

Pocahontas and her father walked out into the bright sunlight. They strolled along the paths between the gardens. Women were picking corn and other vegetables.

Some of the women paused in their work

as they knelt in the gardens. They watched the chief with his muscular shoulders hold one of his daughter's delicate hands.

Pocahontas heard one woman say to another, "Pocahontas is very lucky. Her father loves her very much."

"She's his favorite daughter," the other said.

"And someday she will be a great leader like he is," whispered another, just loud enough for Pocahontas to hear.

Pocahontas strutted very proudly beside her father. She held her head up high, and her eyes shone brightly. She smiled at everyone.

Powhatan said "hello" to people as he and Pocahontas passed by them. They smiled at their fair-minded, courageous leader whom they respected very much.

Powhatan asked a woman if her son was

feeling better. He had been sick.

"Isn't it wonderful that your grandchild will be born soon?" he asked another woman.

Powhatan led Pocahontas away from the gardens and the houses and into the forest.

"That's the direction I take to the English village, when you send me with food." Pocahontas pointed down a path leading to the right.

"I know," her father replied.

The sun warmed them as it filtered down between the pine trees and the bare branches of the other trees losing their leaves.

"I love this land," Powhatan said. "I am part of this land, and my love for this place is my love for my people. It is my duty to make sure my land and my people are safe and well. Do you understand?"

"Yes, Father."

"It is your duty to understand. That is what

you have been chosen to do in life. That is why the gods have made you so smart and alert—and good-hearted," Powhatan said.

"Thank you, Father."

"You must pay attention to the needs of the people, as I do. You must think about what they need to be strong. You are the daughter of the chief. You must observe what everyone is doing and keep them courageous. Your job in life is a spiritual one."

Pocahontas heard some rustling in the trees. She peeked through the leaves and saw a doe with her fawn. Pocahontas silently motioned to her father to look. They stood very still as they watched the two deer eat.

The doe lifted her head and looked at Pocahontas. She seemed as curious about Pocahontas as Pocahontas was about her.

Powhatan led Pocahontas to a temple on a hill overlooking the village. Together they

entered. A high platform held the preserved bodies of dead *werowances*.

Beside the mummies was the statue of the god who guarded the tomb of the former leaders.

"Often I come here to commune with the spirit of my father and pray for wisdom," Powhatan said.

"Did he fight against the English?" Pocahontas asked.

"No, he fought with Spanish missionaries who came here to convert us all to their religion. They came here a long time before the English."

"What happened?"

"We forced them to leave, so we could still worship our own gods. All people must be free to be themselves. Everyone in his own land."

"But it is wonderful to see people from other lands," Pocahontas said.

"Perhaps," Powhatan said. "I, too, am curious about the English."

"Maybe they will take us to see their land one day," Pocahontas said.

Powhatan laughed. "I will stay here."

"I hope the English are safe here. There are not many of them, and they do not live as well as we do. They have almost nothing to eat. We have so much."

Pocahontas and her father left the tomb and headed back down the hill to the village.

People were ready for the feast. The women had finished painting their bodies.

A group of young people with white feathers in their hair were dancing around in a circle. They shook their gourds. The gourds rattled loudly because of the dry seeds inside them.

Powhatan saw messengers from his brother's tribe coming up the path.

"Let's go inside and wait for them to come to us," Powhatan said to Pocahontas. "It won't be long now before I get to satisfy my curiosity about this Englishman."

"And I will see the first Englishman to visit your longhouse!" Pocahontas said.

Inside, a fire was blazing. The smoke drifted out through holes in the roof.

All the women and children of the royal family were sitting on benches behind the row of elders of the tribe. They looked very bright and rich in their paint, feathers, and capes made of animal skins.

Powhatan put on his fine raccoon robe. He took his place in the middle of the row of elders. Directly behind him, Pocahontas took her seat in the row of royal women and children.

All the people wore white feathers in their hair, but Pocahontas had forgotten hers! She jumped out of her seat and ran to her sleeping mat at the other end of the longhouse. She reached underneath it to get her beautiful white feathers.

She tucked them into her headband decorated with shells, adding them to her father's brown turkey feather. Then she ran back to her seat.

Uncle Opechancanough soon came through the door of the longhouse. He and Powhatan greeted each other by placing their left hands over their hearts and raising their right arms.

The English colonists believed this gesture meant "I am your friend" or "I speak the truth."

With Opechancanough came two old men in deerskin clothes, raccoon capes, and feather hair decorations. Between them stood a tall white man.

Opechancanough stepped aside so that Powhatan could see the stranger easily.

He had dark muttonchop whiskers and a twirled mustache. His hair was swept back straight from a point in the middle of his forehead.

His body was completely swaddled in soft cloth instead of fur.

The Englishman held his head high. He looked Powhatan straight in the eyes.

Powhatan's chin was held high, too. With his bony cheeks, strong nose, and wide mouth, Powhatan looked very regal and important.

He gazed down at the Englishman from his perch on the high bench.

Pocahontas could see that the handsome, pale man wasn't a bit afraid. But she herself was shocked to see who it was.

She gave a little cry. "Oh!" It was her

friend, Captain John Smith. She had been visiting him in the English colony since spring.

He had laughed merrily when she scampered up and down trees and ran races faster than the English boys.

She had led Captain John Smith on walks in the woods and shown him where the good berries grew.

She had also shown him which berries would make him sick.

She had taught him the names of food in her Algonquian language, and he had taught her the English names. He was the only Englishman in his village who tried to speak her language.

She had learned English more quickly than he had learned Algonquian, but somehow they had managed to understand each other.

He had taught her that the English called their little settlement Jamestown in honor of their King James far across the ocean.

When she had gone to the chief's room in the longhouse and told Powhatan all these things, Powhatan had said, "Tell him that he calls the settlement Jamestown. But it is part of the Powhatan Confederacy. The land belongs to me."

Now she leaned over and whispered in her father's ear.

"That's my friend! He's the one who welcomes me when I bring food to the English village!"

The Settlers

POCAHONTAS RECALLED the day Captain John Smith and the English had arrived in Powhatan land. She had seen three big English ships with their high wooden masts and brilliant white sails come close to the shore. She had never seen boats like these before.

Indian men made heavy canoes out of big trees to go fishing in the rough waters of the Atlantic Ocean. They also built lightweight birch bark canoes for fishing and traveling on the inland rivers. The Indians could easily carry them overland.

All the canoes were finely crafted. But her people never made them big enough for a man to walk around on, or cook or sleep in. They never had sails made out of cloth. They didn't have any sails at all, not even ones made of animal skin. She thought the English ships were a miracle.

Pocahontas saw many people coming out of the ships. They were very light-skinned people—men, women, and children. And their clothes covered their bodies completely. Their clothes, like their ships, amazed her.

Pocahontas had always been free to roam wherever she pleased on her father's land. Her father didn't know it, but she had often traveled far away from the village.

Now she knew she would have to tell her father how far she had trekked on this bright day in April, 1607.

Pocahontas moved as close as she could

get to the English and their ships without coming out of her hiding place behind some trees. Soon the sun began to set. Pocahontas knew she should go home, but she was too curious to leave her spot.

She watched the people unload big packages from the ships. As dusk fell, they lit a fire by the shore and cooked their food.

Pocahontas headed back into the woods. Moonlight was all she needed to find her way to her father's village. She woke Powhatan and told him what she had seen.

"So the English have come back to try again," Powhatan said calmly. "Keep an eye on them and tell me what they do."

"Yes, Father. I am glad you aren't angry with me for going so far away from home."

"You may go where you wish, Pocahontas," he said. "All of our people know you are my daughter, so you are always safe on my land.

And I don't think the English will harm a child who comes without any weapons."

The next day Pocahontas retraced her steps to the group of English who had camped on the banks of the James River. Captain John Smith, the man who would later become her friend, was among the group. With the help of many other men, he began to build shelters.

Pocahontas watched with fascination. In Indian towns, women built the houses. They bent over the saplings, put up bark walls, and set reed mats down on the floors inside.

But the men took charge of building the English village. The women watched the children and prepared the food.

A small group of men set out from the camp and headed into the woods. Later Pocahontas found out that they met some Indians from the village of Kecoughtan. The

Indians took the English to their village and celebrated with a feast in their honor.

The English had heard that Indians loved glass beads, bells, needles, and other tools and decorations. They gave these things to the Indians as gifts to signal their good will.

That evening, when Pocahontas returned to Werowocomoco, she told her father what she had seen. "The English are building square homes out of wood. They are cutting down trees."

"So far there is peace, but keep watching them," Powhatan said.

Pocahontas kept going back every few days to watch the English. She had many hiding places. Sometimes Pocahontas sat on a hill, or behind a tree, or even in a tree. No one ever saw her.

In just a short while the English colony grew on the bank of the James River. There were about a hundred people and many of them had houses to live in.

The English weren't going to take their boats away quickly. They had even dug up patches of ground to plant food.

One day the *werowance* of a nearby village arrived to pay a visit. He brought many warriors with him. They were very quiet and still, but Pocahontas saw that they carried bows and arrows. She crept closer to get a better look and to hear what they said.

Pocahontas could tell the English were scared. They probably thought the Indians had come to start a fight. Instead, though, the Indians offered a deer for the English to eat.

They ate the food right away. There wasn't any left over to store.

"We will give you more food," the *werowance* said in Algonquian. "In return we ask for tools and beads."

Pocahontas could hear what the *werowance* said, but the English people didn't understand him. Suddenly, one of the Indian men ran forward and grabbed a hatchet. The English drew their swords and firearms and threatened the Indians to get the hatchet back.

"What have you done?" Pocahontas heard the *werowance* yell at the man. "Now they will be afraid and won't trade with us."

The English didn't know what he was saying, but the *werowance* ordered his warriors to leave.

Pocahontas ran to tell her father everything she saw.

"Yes, my messengers bring me such news from many villages," Powhatan said. "The English do not know how to hunt or fish very well. They have planted food, but it will take time for it to grow. So they trade goods with our people in return for food. The Indians are giving them a lot of corn because it is so plentiful this year."

"They are managing to stay alive. That is wonderful," said Pocahontas.

"But I don't like to see them planting food. That means they are going to stay a long time."

"I will find out their plans," Pocahontas promised her father. "I will talk to the English."

Captain John Smith

POCAHONTAS CREPT low under the brush. She was right next to the English village when she saw four boys playing. They were climbing trees and turning cartwheels. They looked to be about her age.

Pocahontas stepped into the open. The boys stared at her. They were surprised to see her.

She walked over to the biggest tree and started to climb. She climbed higher than any of them had.

"Hey!" one little boy said. "Wait for me."

He followed Pocahontas up the tree. The other boys did the same. Pocahontas giggled.

She knew she was a better climber than they were.

Pocahontas touched the very tip of the tree and started scampering back down. She jumped off the last branch, landing softly in the grass. She smiled up at the boys, who were still trying to reach the top.

Suddenly, a man walked over to her.

"Who is this?" he asked. "Why, it's a child. Just a little girl."

Pocahontas stared curiously at the strange-looking man. He had whiskers that stuck out stiffly from his face. He was wearing boots and tight long breeches. The sleeves of his shirt were rolled up. Pocahontas saw he had arm muscles as big as her father's.

Pocahontas wanted to run away. She was afraid. But she didn't move. She stared in his face and noticed he had good eyes. There was no evil or anger in them.

The man was looking just as intently at her. She wondered what he thought. Everyone told her she was pretty, with her long black hair. She was wearing her favorite headband decorated with colorful beads.

Pocahontas didn't understand what he said, but she smiled at him brightly. He smiled back. Like some of her older brothers, he had little creases at the sides of his eyes. She knew he must be at least twice as old as she was.

He pointed at her with a questioning look on his face.

"I'm Pocahontas, the daughter of the great *werowance*, the most powerful chief in the land, Powhatan," she told him.

Smith seemed to understand a little. He recognized the name Powhatan because he had heard it from other Indians.

"I've heard of the great chief Powhatan.

Are you one of his children?"

Pocahontas pointed to herself and said her name again. "I am Pocahontas. Powhatan is my father."

"Pocahontas," Smith repeated. "Powhatan."

She smiled and nodded. He smiled and pointed to himself, "Captain John Smith."

"Captain John Smith."

He clapped his hands in appreciation. She clapped hers to join him in his fun. He laughed at her alertness and curiosity.

Pocahontas rubbed her stomach and pretended to be eating. She then pointed at his stomach and mouth. Captain Smith realized that Pocahontas knew the English were hungry, that they needed food to stay alive.

"Yes," he nodded.

Pocahontas nodded, too. "My father Powhatan will help you."

Smith took her by the hand and gently led

her into the settlement. "Look what I have found," he called to the other settlers. "She comes from Powhatan's tribe. I think she's his daughter."

Pocahontas stayed close to Captain Smith's side. Everyone was staring at her. When the little children saw her, they giggled and screamed because she looked so different. She couldn't understand what Captain Smith told them, but it made them stop.

Pocahontas smiled up at Smith, and he at her. She tried to look deeply into his heart, for she had no other way of telling him that she wanted to be friends.

"You're a very special girl," Captain Smith said to her.

Pocahontas decided to try to teach Captain Smith some Algonquian words. She pointed to a tree and said the Algonquian name. He repeated it and said the name in English.

Slowly, they went around the village pointing at objects, calling out their names in English and Algonquian.

They taught each other the words for corn, berries, and deer meat. Captain Smith taught her the English word, *bed*. She had never seen one before.

By the time Pocahontas was ready to go back home to Werowocomoco that evening, she knew how to say "I bring deer and corn."

Captain Smith gave her a necklace of beads to wear. She skipped off into the woods alone. In one day, and with few words, they had won each other's respect.

She returned soon after the next sunrise. This time she brought four warriors with her. They carried baskets of corn and small game hanging from poles.

Captain Smith said to her, "I know we're safe now that you're here."

New Friends

THE ENGLISH people came up to Pocahontas to thank her for bringing food. They let her roam around the village wherever she wanted, though Captain Smith stayed with her most of the day.

The English were working hard to build their little village. There was a row of houses made from branches woven together. Mud had been smeared over the branches to keep out the wind.

Around the entire village was a wall made of poles. Sharp points, like arrowheads, had been carved out of the top of each pole.

She walked into the woods and watched two men nail a white sail from one of the ships to several trees. Then she saw men, women, and children kneel under the sail. She understood they were praying.

Smith took her close to the group. "They're praying to Jesus Christ," he explained.

Pocahontas nodded. "Praying," she said, her eyes alight and as bright as berries shining with the morning dew still on them.

When they were done praying, the kids came over to meet her. She couldn't understand what they said, but through sign language she knew they were asking her to come play with them.

Pocahontas giggled and nodded yes. She followed them to an open area in the center of the village.

The children put her in a line with them

while one little boy ran and showed her a spot about three houses away. She knew what they were doing. They wanted to have a race! Pocahontas loved to race, especially since she was the fastest girl in her village and faster than most of the boys.

A little girl shouted "Go!" and all the children took off. Pocahontas ran very fast. She was beating all the children except for one little boy. But she didn't give up. She made her legs go even faster.

She whisked by the boy and crossed the finish line first. All the children came running over to congratulate her. Pocahontas smiled proudly. She knew she had made new friends.

"Hooray for Pocahontas!" She turned to see Captain Smith beaming at her. "But why don't you come with me now, and teach me some more words."

He gestured for her to follow him.

Smith sat down with her at a table and wrote down the words that she had taught him in her language. She watched with fascination. He used a feather quill pen and black liquid ink to write on white birch tree bark. Since she did not know how to read and write, she simply remembered all the English words he taught her.

Pocahontas was very tired from her race. Slowly, her eyes began to close.

"I'm sorry to make you work so hard, Pocahontas," Captain Smith said. "Maybe you should take a nap before your journey home."

He took her to a little house that he had built. It had one room with a cooking area, a chair, and a soft bed. He covered her with a blanket, and she fell fast asleep.

Back home, Pocahontas ran to her father.

"I would like an English bed. Will you ask them for an English bed for me?"

"Hmm. What is an English bed?"

"It is high and soft and stuffed with feathers. On top it has a cloth, not an animal skin."

Powhatan sighed. "I have never seen a bed except for my own fine one made of tree branches. It is covered with the softest animal skins. It is the best kind of bed. You don't need an English bed."

"But I would like one, Father."

Powhatan laughed. "Well, we'll see. There are other things we need first."

Pocahontas led trips to the English village many times. Her father's tall, strong men carried the food.

One day she reported back to Powhatan that two of the three ships had left the settlement. Smith had told her that they were returning home. This made Powhatan very happy.

"Good. And when is the last one leaving?" he asked her.

"I don't know," Pocahontas replied.

The next day she asked Smith her father's question. "When is the last ship leaving? Are you going away?"

"Powhatan wants to know," Smith said. "But I don't know the answer."

Pocahontas didn't understand exactly, but she told her father that Captain Smith seemed to know that Powhatan was curious about the English.

By now the leaves were beginning to fall off the trees. Only the pine trees kept their needles.

Days were becoming shorter. The wind grew very cool at night. Soon it would be winter.

The last time Pocahontas visited the English colony with food, she took her little beaver cape to wear on the trip home at night.

It had been two weeks since Pocahontas had been back to the English settlement. Now, suddenly, Captain Smith was standing in her father's longhouse.

She saw that her father and Smith had a similar way of lifting their chins when they talked. Neither man felt afraid of the other. But Captain Smith was Powhatan's prisoner.

Pocahontas felt afraid for Captain Smith. Very afraid.

Pocahontas Risks Her Life

POCAHONTAS WAS astounded to hear her father say an English word: "Peace."

Captain Smith said the same thing. He bowed his head slightly toward Powhatan. When he raised his head again, his stiff, chopped-off chin whiskers seemed to point straight at Powhatan.

Under her breath behind her father, Pocahontas said the word also. "Peace."

Her father looked around at her. "Very good for you. I hope it is true," he whispered. Powhatan turned and focused his stern gaze on the Englishman again.

"I am the *werowance* of the Powhatan Confederacy," Powhatan announced in Algonquian. "The white man calls me by the name Powhatan. What is your name? What are you doing on my land?"

The Englishman stared at Powhatan. "I'm sorry that I don't understand your language very well," he said in English.

The room became silent. The two men stared at each other firmly. Powhatan motioned to one of his wives to bring a plate of nuts and berries forward and hold it out for the Englishman. The Englishman took a few blueberries, said "Thank you" to the woman, and looked back at Powhatan calmly.

He pointed to his chest. "Captain John Smith." Then Captain Smith pointed at Powhatan. "Powhatan."

Powhatan nodded with a proud upward tilt to his head. "Captain John Smith," he repeated, and he motioned Captain Smith to sit down.

Smith lowered himself onto a reed mat directly in front of Powhatan. He sat among a crowd of Indian men.

Seated on his high bench, Powhatan's head was far above everyone else's in the longhouse. He turned slightly toward Pocahontas.

"Captain John Smith is my friend," she whispered. "He is one of the chiefs at Jamestown. He's the kind one."

"And we are kind to him," her father whispered back.

Powhatan turned back toward Captain Smith. "We will now start the feast," he announced.

He waved his hands in the air, and the women brought forward platters of steaming food.

Captain Smith's eyes widened at the plentiful food. He gave Powhatan a broad smile, but Powhatan didn't smile back.

Pocahontas noticed how Smith's face lit up at the sight of all the food. She started to relax. Maybe nothing bad would happen after all.

Smith's smile had always made Pocahontas feel better. He had white, even teeth that were as bright as the animals' teeth the braves polished with sand. The braves wore the teeth as ornaments.

She had never seen so many teeth in a grown man. All the Indians had teeth missing by the time they had grown as tall as Captain Smith.

He had one gleaming metal tooth, too, on the upper right hand side of his mouth. She knew it was gold because Smith had told her so. It reminded her of the shining sun.

A woman brought a bowl made of smooth clay filled with water for Captain Smith to wash his hands. Then she gave him some feathers to dry his hands. The feathers served as towels.

More women brought bowls of steaming corn and clams to Smith and Powhatan. After the men finished these, the women brought them big, deep bowls filled with cornmeal, squash, pumpkin, and deer venison fragrant with herbs. The women also brought clay bowls filled with milky juice to Captain Smith and Powhatan. This juice was made from crushed walnuts. Everyone else was served after them.

While they ate, Powhatan asked the Indians: "Does anyone know Captain John Smith's language? He must understand everything I say."

One of the old Indian men who had come

with Powhatan's brother spoke up. "I will try." He turned to Smith. "Why you here?" He pointed at the ground.

Smith looked at Powhatan as he spoke. "I was hunting for food, when I was captured by your people. I don't understand why your people are afraid of me—and the arrows in my compass."

Captain Smith took out a little round, flat object with arrows on it. "This is just a compass that tells directions so I don't get lost. It can't hurt anybody."

Right away Pocahontas understood that Captain Smith never meant to harm her people. He was only trying to help his own people.

"He is only looking for food," she whispered into her father's ear.

"I understand that," Powhatan said. "But that is what he wants today. Tomorrow he may want all my land."

Powhatan shouted an order to his people. Pocahontas watched in horror as several men seated around Captain Smith jumped up. They brought two big stones from the side of the longhouse to the middle of the room and set them down, one atop the other. The men forced Captain Smith to lie down on the ground. They put his head on top of the stones and held him there.

Two more men jumped down from the bench near Powhatan, holding heavy wooden clubs above Captain Smith's head. Their eyes glinted fiercely at him. He closed his eyes.

Pocahontas couldn't watch this. She jumped from her seat and lay down on top of Captain Smith, her head shielding his. He opened his eyes to see her. She looked into his eyes. She knew they couldn't kill him without killing her, too.

Everyone was shouting. Powhatan's voice,

louder than anyone else's, yelled for the men to put down their clubs.

Pocahontas stood back up and took her place again on the bench behind her father. She kept her eyes cast down at the ground, afraid to look at her father's face.

Captain Smith stood also. Several young men were pointing their bows and arrows at him, but Powhatan told them to put their weapons down.

Captain Smith held very still and looked at Powhatan. Everyone was silent.

"Why have the English come to Powhatan land?" Powhatan asked through the interpreter. "Are you planning to stay forever?"

"No," Captain Smith replied cautiously. He was still scared after what had just happened. "My friends and I have sailed here in search of a way to the other side of the world—to the Indies. Our ship was damaged during the voyage. We can't leave. So we're waiting for another ship to arrive and take us back to England."

The interpreter finished repeating in Algonquian what Captain Smith said, and all the tribe's nobles started shouting. Powhatan ordered everyone to be quiet. He stared silently at Captain Smith.

Pocahontas leaned forward. "He is a stranger here, Father. Please be kind. Maybe he will tell us about his world across the sea."

Powhatan tried to look sternly at her, but his eyes softened when he saw how concerned she was. "Your breath is tickling my ear. Get back. I, too, am curious. But I don't believe a word he says."

"What are you going to do?" Pocahontas asked.

Powhatan turned to the interpreter. "Tell him that I would like to trade with him."

Smith listened to the translation. "I'd be honored to trade with you."

"We will supply you with food, so that you can survive the winter that is coming soon. In return, I want guns such as the one you carry with you now. I want hatchets, too, to cut down trees, and metal pots and tools for building and cooking. And for Pocahontas I want colorful beads."

"That will be fine. I agree to your deal."

"Then smoke some of our tobacco. The pipe means that we want to be peaceful. Four of my men will escort you to your settlement at Jamestown. Send my men back to me safely, and we will begin our trading."

"I am very grateful to you." Captain Smith smiled at Pocahontas. "And also to your daughter. She is always welcome at Jamestown.

"I offer her and your men my protection,

just as you have offered me yours. I shall call you father while I am in your country. I will be your obedient son."

"Pocahontas will come to see you for me," Powhatan said.

Pocahontas sat up very tall and proud.

"I would like to make you a gift of some land near Werowocomoco," Powhatan continued. "You and your people can come to live on this land near me and pay tribute to me. In return you will receive my protection. This is the arrangement I have with all the tribes in the Powhatan Confederacy. And I will also give you a new name. I will call you *Nantaquoud*, and you will be like one of my sons."

"I am honored by your offer, but I cannot accept," Captain Smith replied. "We have already done so much building where we are. It is near the river. We like it there. But I will call you my father while I am in your land."

Powhatan nodded his acceptance. Captain Smith set out with four men from the Powhatan tribe to make his way back from Werowocomoco to the English colony at Jamestown.

Captain Smith always thought that Pocahontas saved his life that day. Much later, however, people who studied Powhatan Indian life came to think that the threatened execution scene was never genuine. It may have been a ritual by which Powhatan welcomed Captain Smith into the tribe, or it might have been just a hoax.

Pocahontas had many questions to ask her father after Captain Smith left. "Do you think he will trade you the gun at his waist in exchange for food?"

"If he doesn't," Powhatan said, "he may one day have no need for food. But I don't know how much venison it will take to trade for one gun. I am sure I'll have trouble with the English one day. They want to remain independent. They want to keep the land they have chosen for themselves. They might want even more land."

"I hope he will accept corn for an English bed," Pocahontas said, with her eyes lively and her cheeks dimpling as she smiled at her father.

"Oh, you and your English bed, Pocahontas. Sometimes you are a little silly," said Powhatan, "but I forgive you."

Everyone in the tribe stayed up to finish all the food from the feast.

Finally, Pocahontas lay down on her bed of twigs and animal skins. She was exhausted. As she fell asleep to the sound of young men dancing, she realized her father was right. Their beds really were the best ones.

The Great Insult

RIGHT AWAY Pocahontas returned to Jamestown. She was very well liked there now, and nearly everyone came out to greet her.

Pocahontas stood at the head of a large party of Indian braves dressed in their doeskin clothes. All the Indians wore fur capes wrapped around their shoulders. The weather was now chilly even in the daytime. There was even some snow on the ground.

The colonists were shivering in their wool and cotton clothes. They looked at the fur wraps enviously.

The Indians began to unload their supplies. They carried many types of vegetables, nuts, and berries. The Powhatan women had smoked the venison and fish to preserve them for the coming winter. Powhatan had even included fur capes to keep the English warm.

In return, Captain John Smith gave the braves copper pots, ornaments, colorful beads, and metal hatchets for chopping wood. He didn't send any guns, though.

Pocahontas played with the children while the braves walked around the colony. Smith took delight in watching her scamper up and down trees faster than the English boys.

"You are a very strong little person," he said.

Pocahontas giggled. "There is one boy who climbs higher than I do, but he did not come out to play today. Many of my friends did not come out today. Where are they?"

"The water has made them sick," Captain Smith replied. "It's salty at high tide and filled with dirt at low tide."

Pocahontas gasped. "Don't drink the water from the sea! Eat berries instead. And press nuts to get their liquid. I'll show you how."

She put a handful of nuts into a bowl and pounded them with a stone until they became a milky liquid. It was the same drink Captain Smith had shared with Powhatan during the feast.

"I remember this," he said, taking a drink. "I wondered how you made it."

Suddenly, people started running toward the ocean and cheering. Pocahontas turned to see a ship sailing toward the colony.

"What's that?" she asked Smith.

"It's a ship called the *Susan Constant*."

She watched the people coming to shore with all of their belongings.

"Who are all those people?" Pocahontas asked Captain Smith.

"They are from England, and they have decided to live here with us. The ship has also brought more supplies for all of us."

Pocahontas frowned, thinking, "My father will not be happy to hear that more English are coming. I must go home immediately and tell him."

Pocahontas was right. Her father was very angry when he heard more English had arrived. He became even angrier after he looked through the supplies Captain Smith had given him in exchange for the food.

"Where are the guns?" Powhatan shouted.

Pocahontas tried to calm her father. "Captain Smith said you could use these hatchets for cutting down trees. They're much stronger than our stones and wooden clubs."

"Go back and tell him I want the guns he promised me. It seems I cannot trust Captain Smith. I don't believe one word of his talk about a plan to go back to England as soon as a rescue ship arrives. You saw with your own eyes! They are bringing supplies and people here instead! They plan to stay!"

Pocahontas was nearly in tears. She knew her father was right, but she also liked her new friends, especially Captain Smith. He had taught her so many interesting things.

The next day she woke up early. She wanted to give Captain Smith her father's message as soon as she could.

Running through the woods, she tripped over a fallen tree limb. She cried out in pain and also in sadness. Pocahontas felt as if something very bad was about to happen.

When she got to the English village she called out to her friend. "Captain Smith!"

Then she stopped and looked around. Almost everything was gone! A fire had destroyed the storehouse with all of the new supplies from England. Many of the houses had burned down, too. Sails draped over tree limbs were being used for shelters.

Captain Smith saw Pocahontas standing there. "Oh, Pocahontas, I'm so happy to see you. Look at what happened to us. I'll have to beg your father for more help."

"I'll take you to him. But I must warn you. He is very mad at you for not keeping your word."

Pocahontas and Captain Smith set off to see Powhatan. In the longhouse, Powhatan listened to Captain Smith's story in silence.

"The god Okeus has done this. Okeus punishes men for breaking moral laws. You must give us guns. You have promised them in trade. You must keep your word if you do not want to be punished again."

"I promise to send you guns when we get some," Captain Smith said. "We have very few left right now because of the fire. We have very little of everything.

"But we will help defend you in wars against your enemies," Smith added, echoing the promise that Powhatan always made to the chiefs of other tribes.

"Leave me now so I can decide what to do."

Captain Smith said good-bye and headed back to Jamestown.

Pocahontas turned to her father. "They have nothing. I have seen their losses with my own eyes. Without us they will die. Please help them."

"For you, my child, I will help them. But they had better keep their word this time."

Powhatan sent food to the English again. Pocahontas also introduced Captain Smith to chiefs of other Powhatan villages, including one ruled by her half brother, Pochins. Captain Smith and Pochins became close friends, and Pochins sent corn and fish to the English.

The English managed to survive that very cold winter with Pocahontas's help. By learning their language and customs, she was better able to help them trade with the Indians. She also taught them how to catch oysters. Without her, they surely would have starved.

The friendship between Pocahontas and Captain Smith formed a lifeline between the settlers and the Powhatans. And because he had made this strong connection with the Indians just when the settlers needed it most, Smith was elected head of the Jamestown Council, the settlement's governing body.

This was a far cry from the way he had been treated on the ship coming from England. The day the ship had arrived, Smith was actually in chains below deck. He had been accused of plotting a mutiny.

The captain had feared the way Smith bragged about his heroism during wars in Europe, before he had sailed to the New World. But once the ship landed, Smith had been quickly released and named to the governing council, according to the king of England's written orders.

Smith was a born leader. He liked to present himself as a fearless tough man, confident and worthy of respect from everyone. In the end, he didn't have to force the colony to choose him as its leader. The settlers did it of their own free will.

That spring Pocahontas continued her trips to Jamestown. But during the summer, she noticed that her father and the elders of the tribe seemed worried. There had not been enough rain, so there would not be very much food to last them through the winter. If if didn't rain soon, there might not be any food to trade with the English.

Pocahontas decided to visit Captain Smith and her English friends to see how they were doing. Maybe they would not need as much help as before.

When Pocahontas arrived in Jamestown, she noticed a ship anchored in the bay.

"Are more people arriving?" she asked Captain Smith.

"That's the *Susan Constant*, the ship that arrived last fall. It went back to England and has now returned with more supplies," Captain Smith said. "Lord Newport is its captain. I have told him all about you. He is looking forward to meeting you."

Captain Smith led Pocahontas to a table where Lord Newport was looking over some maps. "Lord Newport, I would like to introduce you to Pocahontas, the daughter of Chief Powhatan."

Lord Newport smiled at her as he extended his hand to shake hers. "It's a pleasure to finally meet you. Captain Smith has told me many wonderful things about you and your people."

"It is nice to meet you, too, Lord Newport," Pocahontas said. "I enjoy meeting all the English people who come here."

"I have also heard many things about your father," Lord Newport continued. "I would be honored if you would ask him if I could come to visit him sometime soon. I have brought gifts from my king, King James."

"I will ask my father tonight. I'm sure he will say yes."

Pocahontas ran to her father as soon as she got back home.

"Father, Father! There is a new man in Jamestown. His name is Lord Newport, and he would like to meet you and give you gifts from his king."

Powhatan was very pleased. "Finally the English are bringing us guns. They have decided to give us what we want in return for all we have given them. Tell him he may visit me."

Pocahontas was very excited. Captain Smith was going to bring Lord Newport to Werowocomoco in two days. She hoped that her father would like Lord Newport. Then the English and the Powhatans would get along better.

Finally, the day of Lord Newport's visit arrived. "Come, Pocahontas," her father called to her. "We will wait for them in the longhouse. I want you beside me to tell me what they say."

"Yes, Father. I will enjoy doing that for you very much."

Pocahontas could hardly sit still, waiting for them to arrive. Then she heard her friends' voices.

First Captain Smith entered, followed by Lord Newport and two other men from the English village. Powhatan rose from his seat as Captain Smith and Lord Newport stood before him.

"Thank you for seeing us, Chief Powhatan." Captain Smith made the same gesture he had seen Powhatan and Opechancanough make the first time he had met Powhatan. He placed his left hand on his heart and raised his right arm. Lord Newport did the same thing.

"Chief Powhatan," Lord Newport said. "I am Lord Newport. I have just arrived in your beautiful land from England. In honor of the kindness and generosity you have shown my people, I offer you these gifts on behalf of King James."

Lord Newport stepped back and swept his right arm behind him. One of the men who had come with him stepped forward. He was carrying a long, beautiful red robe and a crown made of copper.

Powhatan looked at them in confusion. He did not understand why they were giving him these strange gifts. Where were the guns he had asked for?

"Please, sir, let me help you." Lord Newport took the robe from the man's arms and stepped up to Chief Powhatan. He wrapped the rope around the chief's shoulders. Then he took the crown and placed it on Chief Powhatan's head.

"By the authority of King James, I now pronounce you Emperor Powhatan of the

90

Powhatans." Lord Newport bowed low to Powhatan.

Pocahontas watched her father grow angrier and angrier as she repeated these words in Algonquian.

Powhatan grabbed the crown off his head and threw it on the ground. "What gives you the right to make me emperor! I already am the *werowance* of all the Powhatans. I do not need the English king to tell me who I am! You were supposed to bring me the guns you owe me. Leave now, before I have you all taken prisoner."

Powhatan pointed toward the door as he glared down at Lord Newport and Captain Smith.

"We had better go," Captain Smith said, pulling Lord Newport toward the door.

Pocahontas could not believe what she had seen. How could the English have done that to her father? He was a proud leader. He would never stand for such an insult.

"Father," she pleaded, "they must have made a mistake. Lord Newport must not have known what gifts you were expecting to receive."

"Oh, my sweet, trusting child. That was no mistake. The English meant to belittle me. They want our land and our souls."

"I can't believe that. Captain Smith is such a good, honorable man. He is my friend." She looked pleadingly into her father's eyes. "Please, let me talk to him. I'm sure I can make things better between you."

"I will give him one more chance. If he does not give you the guns the next time you bring him food, I will have to decide what to do with Captain John Smith."

Saying Good-bye

THE NEXT time Pocahontas went to see Captain Smith, she asked him about the guns. But Captain Smith told her that he had no guns to trade. Pocahontas dreaded giving her father this news. She knew he would not be happy.

"I do not trust Captain Smith," he told her. "I do not believe that they have no guns."

Winter was once again setting in, and it promised to be an especially fierce one. The journey to the English village was becoming difficult for Pocahontas. But she wrapped her beaver cape tightly around her shoulders and braved the cold. She had to make sure her English friends were all right.

After one difficult trip, she noticed Captain Smith looked very pale and sickly.

"I must speak to your father," he said with a hoarse voice. "We have no food. We are starving. I must ask Chief Powhatan for help."

"We have barely enough food for ourselves. But I will take you to him."

Pocahontas took Captain Smith back to her village and led him to Chief Powhatan's private room in the longhouse. The chief was eating smoked fish with a glistening skin and a glittery eye which his wives had served him. Smith told him that he needed food for his people.

"Wait here," Powhatan said. "I must ask the elders for advice. You come with me, Pocahontas." In the middle of the longhouse, he gathered the elders of the tribe together.

Pocahontas was now thirteen years old.

She was dressed in the traditional doeskin clothes worn by all adult Powhatans. She no longer climbed trees, turned cartwheels, or ran races. She was starting to feel very grown-up.

Pocahontas took a seat next to her father on a raised platform above the elders. Smith couldn't hear any of the conversation. Powhatan came straight to the point.

"Captain Smith has come to ask for more food. But he never keeps his word. I've put up with this as long as I can. I want a party of my best warriors to kill Smith tonight. Then I will trade with someone else at Jamestown who will give me what I want.

"Perhaps Lord Newport will keep his word, and I will get some guns. I am sick of the delay. I don't want more and more English coming here every year and never giving me what I ask for."

He chose a small group of braves to carry out the assassination. They were to stay in Werowocomoco, where Smith was told to wait overnight for the food. They were to kill Smith and then rejoin the tribe, which was going to leave Werowocomoco right away.

The Indians were moving to a place where they could hunt for game and survive the long winter.

Pocahontas was stunned. "Please think again, Father. Captain Smith is my friend. I know he respects you."

"No! He does not respect us. He wants our land for his king."

Pocahontas tried to keep her voice calm. "There are thousands of us in all our tribes. Even though the English have guns, they can't take our lands. There are only a few hundred English people. All of us could defend our land. You are so powerful. We must not be afraid of the few strangers among us."

Powhatan shook his head. "He breaks his promises. We cannot trust him."

"The English have another king. You have always told me we must respect the ways of others. This is very important."

Powhatan stood. "I will tell Captain Smith we will give him some food."

He looked down at his daughter's sad eyes with kindness. "I understand you are sad because you and Captain Smith are friends. But you must understand something, too. Trouble will befall us all if I let his lies continue. Now all of us must get ready to leave."

Pocahontas did as she was told. She packed her belongings. With a heavy heart, she watched the women take apart the houses.

Pocahontas knew she had to save her friend. She followed the tribe as it started the journey. But soon she dropped behind and sneaked back to Werowocomoco. There she found Captain Smith and whispered to him about the danger.

"Take care for your life. My father has sent a party of braves to kill you. Be warned, and promise me that you will do nothing to harm my father in revenge."

"I promise," he said. "What will happen to you if your father finds out you have come back here to warn me, Pocahontas? I'm afraid for your safety. Do you want to stay with me?"

"No. I must go back to my tribe," she said. "All my blessings have always come to me from my father and our great people."

"You are my dearest friend, Pocahontas. Will you take some copper and beads? I want to show my gratitude."

"No, I can't be seen with such things. If my father finds out what I have done, I could die. I must run now. I hope we will meet again soon."

She fled back to her tribe. John Smith stayed up all night in the Indian village. He stayed alert and was able to avoid harm.

Smith returned to Jamestown. He told Lord Newport, "That was a close call. We can no longer depend so heavily on the Indians.

Our colony must learn to take care of itself."

Smith ordered the people to work harder. They hated the constant work, but they ended up making the fort bigger and stronger. They even deepened the well to get more water that was drinkable. Because of all their hard work, the settlers managed to survive that cold winter.

During the next summer, in 1609, Smith saw a sail on the horizon. A ship captained by a man named Samuel Argall, a veteran English seaman, arrived.

Argall brought supplies, and he also brought plenty of news. A group of wealthy English nobles had taken over the financial support of the colonies. They had enough money to help the colonists continue their effort on a grand scale. More supplies and people would be arriving soon.

"I'm delighted to hear this," Captain Smith

said to Argall. "We need the help."

"Yes. This is great news for the colony," Argall said. "But I have some bad news for you personally. These noblemen have decided to replace you as governor of the colony. They have chosen instead another nobleman, Lord de la Warr."

"What?" Captain Smith shouted. "How could they do this? De la Warr is to become head of the governing council? And what am I supposed to do?"

"I believe you will be allowed to remain on the council," Argall replied. "But I'm not sure."

Smith's eyes flashed at Argall. "What are you talking about? After all I've done for this colony and for England, now I'm just to be thrown away? This is a terrible insult!"

"I'm sure you are expected to help out with the settlement," Argall continued. "You know how to speak with the Indians and have such good relations with them. You will simply give up leading the colony."

"I can't and I won't," Smith said.

Smith packed his belongings and left the colony. For a while he stayed with a Powhatan Indian named Parahunt, one of Pocahontas's half-brothers. Smith was going to settle on some land that Parahunt had given him, but a bag of gunpowder accidentally exploded, burning Smith very badly. He was forced to return to Jamestown for medical treatment.

In Jamestown, however, life for Smith did not get any better. His burns were so severe that the doctor there could not treat them. Even more important, the settlers were very angry with him for the hard work he had made them do. They also accused him of plotting to marry Pocahontas so that he could inherit her father's land, which included Jamestown.

Smith and his supporters denied these charges. Smith and Pocahontas respected each other greatly, but they were never planning to get married. At this time, Smith didn't even know where she was.

Smith won this argument, but he still decided it was time to return to England. He was not as respected by the colonists as he had once been, and his burns needed to be looked at by a doctor.

In October 1609, Smith boarded a ship leaving for England. He didn't send word to Pocahontas or any of his Indian friends that he was leaving. Governor Percy, the acting governor until Lord de la Warr arrived, spread the rumor to the Indians that Captain Smith had died. Several of Powhatan's braves heard the story and told Powhatan. Pocahontas also heard the rumor.

Kidnapped!

POWHATAN NEVER found out that Pocahontas had warned Smith. But after that time, relations between the father and daughter became strained.

"I want to go to visit the tribal city of Potomac and stay with my brother Pasptanze there," Pocahontas told her father.

"It's far away. It's one of the most distant villages," her father said.

Pocahontas sighed heavily. "Yes, but it is also very peaceful."

"That's true, but you have never been so far away from me before."

"I want to live in a quiet place."

Powhatan said, "Perhaps it is time. I will let you go. Yes."

"Thank you, Father," Pocahontas said.

Pocahontas began to walk away.

Then he called after her. "Pocahontas, tell yourself that the sky is blue, the grass is green, and the rivers run clear, and you can see the fish. Then you will find peace."

"Thank you, Father."

Pocahontas settled into her new life in Potomac. As the sister of the chief, she received as much respect as she had in her own village.

Much of her time was spent as it would have been at home: preparing food and helping keep the little ones occupied during the long winter months. She taught them games to play and songs to sing.

She was also adding more beaver skins to

her cape. In the last year, she had grown much taller. Her cape was too small to keep her warm.

Pocahontas was also old enough now to join the women of the tribe and paint designs on her body. Bright, beautiful designs covered almost her entire body.

She enjoyed her peaceful life, but she missed her father and the long talks they used to have. Many times she would think of her English friends, too, especially Captain Smith, and wonder how they were doing. No one ever sent word to her. She hoped they were surviving the long, cold winter.

Months passed and finally spring, and then summer, arrived. One day while Pocahontas was out picking berries, her brother Pasptanze came over to talk to her.

"Pocahontas, I have just received a messenger from our father Chief Powhatan.

He has brought news of your friend, Captain Smith."

Pocahontas stopped what she was doing and looked up at him. "Oh, please tell me what he said!"

"He told me Captain Smith is dead."

"No! He can't be." Pocahontas sank to her knees. "How did this happen?"

"No one knows." Pasptanze placed his hand on Pocahontas's shoulder. "Please do not be too sad, Sister. We will all miss Captain Smith."

Pocahontas couldn't bring herself to believe Captain Smith was dead. But months passed with still no word from him. She began to think he really must be dead.

A young brave in her brother's tribe, Kocoum, wanted to marry her. Pocahontas considered marrying him. But when she thought about how routine her life would be, it made her very sad. She longed for the exciting days of visiting Jamestown and her friend Captain Smith.

Word came to Pocahontas, too, about the hard winter at Jamestown. Powhatan had sent orders for her to stay away from the colony. Without her help, the English had not been able to trade with Powhatan. Her father refused to deal with them without Pocahontas there to talk him into it.

Chief Powhatan had forbidden all his tribes to trade with the English. So after the new supplies ran out, there was very little food in Jamestown again.

Years passed. Pocahontas was a lovely young woman now.

One day she saw a small British boat coming toward her brother's village. She couldn't believe her eyes. She thought it was just a mirage. Seeing it reminded her of the first time she had spied an English ship.

She watched it grow larger as it neared. Perhaps Captain Smith was finally coming to see her!

A regal, good-looking man came ashore and walked toward her. "Hello, I am Captain Samuel Argall."

Pocahontas smiled at the sound of the English language. "Hello. I am Pocahontas."

Captain Argall looked surprised to hear English spoken so well by an Indian. But then his face broke out in a smile. "I can't believe my eyes. I have heard so much about you, and here you are!" he said. "Nobody had any idea where you were."

"I live here now," she said. "It's very peaceful."

"And you are all grown up," said Argall.

"Yes, I am eighteen now," she said with a wide smile. Her dark eyes shone with happiness to see someone from Jamestown.

"Do you miss Jamestown?" he asked.

"Sometimes," she said. "But my father doesn't want me to go there. And Captain Smith isn't there, is he?"

"No," Captain Argall said. "He is dead."

"Then it's true. I heard that he had died, but I didn't want to believe it."

"I'm afraid it is true," he said.

"Why have you come to my brother's village?"

"I have come to ask for his help. The settlers in Jamestown are not doing well. They must trade with the Indians if they wish to survive."

"But my father has forbidden any of his chiefs to trade with you."

Captain Argall bowed his head. "I know; that is why I've come to see Pasptanze. I am hoping that, since he is so far away from your father, perhaps he would agree to trade with us."

"Follow me. I'll take you to him."

Pocahontas and Captain Argall walked through the pine trees to the village. They went into Pasptanze's longhouse.

Pasptanze listened to the English captain's story.

"I'll trade one thousand bushels of corn for English goods, your beads and copper pots," said Pasptanze.

Argall said, "I'm so grateful."

But all the time they were talking, a plan to take Pocahontas back to Jamestown was forming in Captain Argall's mind. Then he could tell Powhatan that the English had captured Pocahontas, and Powhatan would be forced to allow the Indians to start trading with the English again.

Argall knew he would need the help of the

Indians, and he knew of an especially friendly couple he could count on. Before leaving Pasptanze's village, Captain Argall spoke to Iapassus and his wife.

"I would like to invite you and your wife to have dinner on my ship before I sail back to Jamestown," Captain Argall said to them.

"We accept your invitation," Iapassus said. He translated for his wife, who smiled at Captain Argall.

Captain Argall said, "I would also like you to do me a favor. Bring Pocahontas with you to dinner."

Iapassus frowned. "I will ask her. But we should ask Pasptanze to come to the ship for dinner also."

"No," Captain Argall said. "I don't think that's a good idea."

"Yes," Iapassus insisted. "I will invite him."

"No, don't do that," Captain Argall said. "I

want Pocahontas to come back to Jamestown with me. I will talk to her after dinner. If Pasptanze is there, he will try to convince her not to go."

"But she has no reason to go to Jamestown. She is very happy here. And her father has forbidden her to go there," Iapassus said.

Captain Argall stared at Iapassus.

"I don't think this is a good plan," Iapassus continued. "My wife and I cannot invite Pocahontas onto your ship like that. We must tell her in advance that you want her to go with you to Jamestown."

Captain Argall smiled at Iapassus. "I'll tell her right after dinner, and I will give you and your wife a copper pot of your very own for doing this favor for me."

Iapassus told his wife they would get a copper pot if they brought Pocahontas to the ship. Quickly they decided.

"Yes, we will do it."

"Thank you," Captain Argall said. He smiled so widely that his mustache stuck out beyond his ears.

Pasptanze threw a great feast for the English that night. The women cooked deer and turkeys and prepared a sauce made from berries. The young men danced in a circle until late at night.

Captain Argall, Pasptanze, and the elders of the tribe smoked a pipe together. Captain Argall coughed from the strong, rough tobacco the Indians used, but he bravely smoked the pipe to show friendship and good faith.

Pocahontas sat behind Pasptanze during the feast, exactly as she had sat behind her father at his feasts. She was obviously an honored member of the village.

During the feast, Iapassus asked Pocahontas to join them on Captain Argall's ship.

"Yes," Pocahontas said. "I would be happy to join you. I have always loved spending time with the English."

The next day, Pocahontas greeted Captain Argall with a smile. "This is the first time I have ever been on a British ship. Thank you for letting me come."

Captain Argall's servant served a big meal while Captain Argall told Pocahontas how much Jamestown had changed.

"We have more buildings and forts, and there are new settlements nearby. One is called Henrico. It is up the river from Jamestown. Many more people are living in the settlements now, so we have built new schools and churches."

"I would love to see Jamestown again one day," Pocahontas said as she yawned sleepily. The big meal had made her tired.

"Are you tired?" Captain Argall asked her.

"Why don't you take a nap before you go back to your village?"

"All right," Pocahontas replied. "I'll close my eyes for just a little while."

Captain Argall, Iapassus, his wife, and Pocahontas walked around the ship, inspecting various parts of it, until they reached a little cabin below the main deck. The cabin was

dark because it had no window. But it did have a comfortable English bed.

Captain Argall left the Indians there, saying, "Enjoy your rest."

Pocahontas lay down on the bed. Iapassus and his wife remained standing.

"We're going to take a walk around the ship again," Iapassus said. "We'll be back for you soon."

They walked out of the cabin. Pocahontas heard a key turn in the lock on the other side of the door.

"Why have they locked the door?" she asked herself.

She went to try to open it. It didn't budge.

"Captain Argall!" she cried, but he didn't come. She sat down on the bed and waited.

Soon she heard people shouting to each other in English. Then the boat began to rock. She knew they were sailing away.

"Oh! I'm a prisoner!" she cried out.

On shore, Iapassus and his wife were holding a big copper pot.

Pocahontas curled up on the bed and waited to see what would happen next. But even before Captain Argall came back to the cabin, Pocahontas knew what was going on. Captain Argall was taking her to Jamestown against her will. He would try to use her to blackmail her father into trading with the English.

"I'm very stupid," she told herself. "I should have known better. I am too trusting sometimes. My father was right. But he is never trusting. That is wrong, too. I knew I could trust John Smith. But Captain Argall is not Captain Smith."

Captain Argall soon came to the cabin, unlocked the door, and entered. He told her what she already knew. She was being taken to Jamestown.

"You will enjoy seeing Jamestown again," Captain Argall said. "You might be so impressed that you will tell Powhatan to look kindly upon us poor colonists. He is holding some of our men captive. We would like them back. And perhaps you can convince Powhatan to trade with the English again. Then I will personally make sure you get home safely to your father."

Pocahontas sat very still. She knew she was at the mercy of Captain Argall. But she was sure of one thing. Somehow, her father would help her.

Prisoner

IN THE OLD DAYS, Pocahontas had pranced into little Jamestown ahead of the braves and gift bearers. Now she walked alone with her eyes cast down on the ground. She was taken to a house and locked inside. She refused to eat or talk to anyone.

Sir Thomas Gates, the new governor of the colonies of Jamestown and Henrico, came to visit her. He was wearing tight leg breeches, high, buckled shoes, and a long vest with a full skirt that came down to the top of his legs. She barely said hello.

"Your father has refused to trade with us,

and he hasn't permitted any of the other tribes in the Powhatan Confederacy to trade with us, either. The Potomacs are the only Indians who will have anything to do with us. But they are far away. We need your father's cooperation if we are going to survive here. If he agrees to help us, we'll let you go wherever you want. But you will be safe here at all times. No one will harm you, I promise."

Pocahontas said nothing.

"I'm sorry to meet you this way, Pocahontas," Sir Thomas Gates continued. "I know how good you have been to our people. If I could do anything else, I would. Your father is a very stubborn man. But he's a great leader, and he loves you very much. I'm sure he'll send help. And you'll soon be free."

Pocahontas was very sad and impatient. Each day, she waited, and she told herself, "The sun is bright, the grass is green, and the rivers run clear, and you can see the fish." Her father's advice made her feel peaceful.

But it took three months for him to reply. Then he sent back seven Englishmen who had been taken prisoner. With each of them was a broken musket. He supplied only one canoe full of corn. He also sent the message that he would give the English five hundred bushels of corn and make peace with them after they returned Pocahontas.

The English were stunned. Then they realized that Powhatan knew they would never harm Pocahontas. He was willing to gamble on their goodwill toward her. And he didn't feel he had to let himself be blackmailed to save her life. The English would provide her with the best of everything. She was a princess who had served them well.

The wily Powhatan guessed correctly. The English took Pocahontas out of the house where they had jailed her, and they sent her to live on a farm owned by a Christian minister, the Reverend Alexander Whitaker. He respected the Indians. In a sermon he preached that the English and the Indians were equals. All of them had souls and minds. All of them were descended from Adam and Eve.

As a child, Pocahontas had been allowed to wear her own doeskin clothes as she watched

the English going about their tasks. She had been curious to learn their customs.

Now she was forced to join them. The minister instructed her to put away her Indian clothes and beads and feathers in a closet.

She was given a stiff corset made with whalebones. On top of that she put on a blouse that covered her arms and chest all the way up to her neck. She also had to wear an ankle-length skirt.

She was told to bow her head down and look at the ground when she walked in the streets. That was the way Englishwomen had to behave.

But her captors treated her well. Soon she relaxed and got used to her new life.

She spent her days learning to recite the prayers of the Church of England. Reverend Whitaker told everyone that she was a very happy, eager pupil.

Within a few weeks of her arrival at Whitaker's farm, Pocahontas consented to become baptized a Christian. The leaders of the colony were delighted to send a message about her conversion to King James I of England. Here was an Indian princess who wanted to become a member of the English colony.

A crowd turned out to watch Reverend Whitaker baptize Pocahontas. She was given an English name for her baptism. Officially to the English, she became known as Rebecca. Many colonists began to call her by her Christian name.

Still, there was no word from her father about any trade with the English.

A New Life

ONE THING didn't change for Pocahontas. Because of her delightful personality, the English truly liked her. And one Sunday in Reverend Whitaker's church, a slender, quiet man named John Rolfe noticed her. He had never seen her before. He had arrived in Jamestown after she had paid her last visit to Captain John Smith.

John Rolfe had arrived at the colony in 1610. He had left England accompanied by his wife, and they had had a child during the voyage. But both his wife and child died before reaching the New World.

Rolfe was very sad and lonely in Jamestown, so he tried to take comfort in his religion and his work. A farmer by trade, he experimented with growing a new kind of tobacco plant.

His tobacco was similar to the type grown by Spanish settlers in the West Indies. The English found it very agreeable. It didn't burn, scratch, and tickle their noses and throats the way the Indians' tobacco did.

After Rolfe's tobacco took root and flourished, he began sending it to England. It became very popular, and it was a great boon for Rolfe and the economy of the colony. Rolfe was a rich farmer by the time he set eyes on Pocahontas/Rebecca.

He struck up a conversation with her after church. At first he spoke with her because he wanted to show kindness to the stranger in the English colony. Mindful of her background as an Indian princess, he respectfully called her Pocahontas. Then he noticed how lively and intelligent she was. He found himself very attracted to the small, dark woman with delicate hands.

Every free moment he had, John Rolfe visited Pocahontas at Reverend Whitaker's farm. He sat with her in church on Sundays, and he escorted her home. They took walks together in his tobacco fields and talked about the beauty of the land.

Pocahontas liked Rolfe's character. He was a sweet, respectful man. He shared her curiosity about people and places. He was as fond of her land as Captain John Smith had been. Rolfe was about the same age as Captain John Smith had been when she had first met him. Pocahontas thought Rolfe was a fine man.

Rolfe wrote a letter to his friend, Sir Thomas Dale, confiding that he had fallen in love with Pocahontas. Rolfe thought about her all the time. He wanted to marry her. He worried if it was proper for a religious Christian man such as himself to marry a woman who had been born "a heathen."

Sir Thomas Dale was delighted to hear about Rolfe's love for Pocahontas. Dale, too, saw beauty in the Indians and their way of life. Some English people were prejudiced and felt superior to the Indians. But Dale didn't feel that way. He knew the English and Indians distrusted each other because they were struggling for control of the land.

Dale thought a marriage between a colonist and the daughter of the great Indian leader Powhatan could help the colonists in their relations with the Indians.

Dale also thought the people in England would be impressed. They would believe that the English colonists enjoyed wonderful relations with the Indians. The marriage might encourage more people to venture to the New World. And the financial backers of the colony would be inspired to send more money.

Rolfe was relieved to hear that Dale was on his side. Rolfe proposed marriage to Pocahontas. She was happy about the proposal and decided to accept him as her husband. Then Sir Thomas Dale, John Rolfe, and Pocahontas discussed the marriage plans.

"I think we should tell Powhatan," Rolfe said. "We don't want him to be surprised by our marriage. And it's only proper for me to ask permission from the father of my beloved Pocahontas. I want him to bless our marriage."

"That's the best idea," Sir Thomas Dale agreed.

Pocahontas, Rolfe, Dale, and many English friends set sail in the spring of 1614 to see Powhatan. He had moved back to

Werowocomoco. Dropping anchor a few miles from the town, Pocahontas and the English waited for Powhatan to greet them. But he never appeared.

Instead two of Pocahontas's brothers came to find out how their sister was. They had orders to report back about her condition to Powhatan. Pocahontas shocked them, because she was wearing English clothes. Her brothers stared at her. But her face was unchanged. Her eyes were still lively and bright.

"I'm fine," Pocahontas told them. "You can see that. The English have treated me very well. I'm only unhappy that Father never sent corn to the English so that they would have set me free. I was kept a prisoner for a while. Then I felt at home in the colony and accepted the Christian religion.

"Now I live with full freedom among the English. I want to stay with them. I'm not coming back to live in Werowocomoco. But I want to tell father that I intend to marry a colonist named John Rolfe. You see him here with me."

She gestured with one of her delicate hands to the tall, slender farmer standing beside her. Her brothers were astounded and talked to each other in private for a while. Then they decided they should all go to see Powhatan together.

John Rolfe and another Englishman went with the Indians to see Powhatan in person. Powhatan refused to meet them. He would only meet their leader, Sir Thomas Dale, face-to-face. Powhatan told them this through a messenger.

John Rolfe sent a message back with one of Powhatan's trusted assistants. Rolfe said he wanted to marry Pocahontas. Powhatan sent back the message that he approved of the marriage. He also wanted to end the war with

the English. "I'm tired of fighting," he said.

On April 5, 1614, Pocahontas and John Rolfe were married in a church in Jamestown. The bride was nineteen years old. She wore an English wedding dress of fine muslin and a long veil and robe. Around her neck, she wore a string of freshwater pearls. Powhatan had sent them to her as a wedding present.

Pocahontas's uncle, a *werowance* of his own village, and two of her brothers went to the wedding. Powhatan himself refused to go. The English believed that he didn't want to give anyone the impression that he had surrendered his land. He simply wanted to live without wars. He accepted the situation that he could not drive the English away.

The senior minister in Jamestown performed the wedding ceremony.

To show his enduring love, Powhatan gave

Pocahontas and John Rolfe some land north of Jamestown on the James River. The couple built a house there. They named it Varina in honor of the Spanish word for the type of tobacco Rolfe grew.

Once when Sir Thomas Dale was visiting Powhatan, Powhatan asked him how Pocahontas and Rolfe "lived, loved and liked." Dale told Powhatan that the couple was very happy.

Powhatan smiled. "Too many of my own people and too many Englishmen have died. I am old now, and I want to live in peace until the end of my days."

The English and the Powhatans still fought little battles occasionally. But there was no war. They traded with each other again. People referred to the time as the Peace of Pocahontas.

A year after their marriage, Pocahontas

and John Rolfe had a baby son, whom they named Thomas, probably in honor of Sir Thomas Dale. The financial backers of Jamestown were so delighted that they set up a financial award to be paid every year to Pocahontas and her son. The money was their way of thanking her for all the help she had given the colony.

For more than half her life, Pocahontas had followed her heart to keep peace between the Indians and the English. Her father had rewarded her with land of her own. And the couple lived freely and happily.

The Great Journey

ALL THE children in Jamestown and Henrico went to schools run by ministers of the Church of England. The schools had few luxuries or supplies. More students arrived on each boat.

The king of England had always wanted the English settlers to convert the Indians to Christianity. That was one of the king's main goals. So far Pocahontas was the only convert.

The colonists knew that the best way to convert the Indians was to take them into Christian schools. But there wasn't enough room in their schools. Ministers talked about how wonderful it would be to have enough money to start a big school. All the children could study together.

The clergymen thought of Pocahontas. She was full of energy and quick-witted. She spoke the English language well. She had a dignified manner. And she felt equally comfortable with the English and her own people.

If only the colonists could introduce Pocahontas to the Virginia Company—the backers of the colonies who lived in London. They might send money to the colony for a first-rate Christian school for English and Indian children.

The clergymen decided to visit Pocahontas at Varina and ask if she would go to England and meet with the businessmen at the Virginia Company. Perhaps the Virginia Company could even find a way to present her at the court of King James I. The king might help fund the school.

So one sunny morning, a party of clergymen took a boat and sailed to the farmhouse where Pocahontas/Rebecca Rolfe now lived with her husband and son on the shore of the James River.

They found her singing an Indian lullaby to Thomas. The baby, who was now a year old, gurgled, smiled, and stared up with big, dark eyes at the Englishmen.

Pocahontas had her baby tied to a board—a crib board—in the Indian fashion. She had propped him up against a wall. That way she could keep an eye on him while she did her daily chores.

"Have you ever thought about visiting London?" Reverend Whitaker asked. He was among the handful of clergymen visiting the Rolfe home that day.

Pocahontas smiled, and her eyes brightened. "I used to think it would be wonderful to go there. I told my father I would love to see London. I thought people should have the opportunity to learn about each other's ways."

"And what did your father say?" another minister asked.

"He thought everyone should stay at home. He didn't want to go to England himself. But he was always curious about the English. I think he taught me to be curious and interested in other people's hearts. He is a great student of people and a great teacher about them, too."

"Let us come to the point of our visit," Reverend Whitaker said. "We would like you to go to London and meet the people who support this colony. They are enthusiastic about their investment here. We want them to send money for a Christian school where Indian and English children can study together. If the Virginia Company people meet you, they'll become excited about the school."

"That's a wonderful idea," Pocahontas said. "I'd be honored to go."

"Will John let you go? Or will he go with you?" Reverend Whitaker asked.

"The three of us will go together," Pocahontas said. "I'm sure John would like to see his brother in England."

John Rolfe came back to the house to find the clergymen in the house with Pocahontas. When the clergymen told John what they wanted, Rolfe looked at Pocahontas.

"What does my wife say?" he asked.

"She wants all three of you to go," Reverend Whitaker said.

"So we'll go," said Rolfe with a wide smile. "Give me time to arrange for people to take care of the farm while we're away."

John Rolfe hired three men to take care of the farm. Pocahontas went to her father to ask for moral support and blessings. Powhatan was very happy for her. Above all, he was proud that the English had asked her to go to do business for them.

"So, you are finally going," he said. "You have always wanted to go to London."

"I never thought this dream would come true," she said.

"You must take many of our people with you," her father said. "You must not go alone with your husband and my grandson. You will be very far away. I have no authority in the land of the English king. So I will send a dozen men and women with you for your protection. I will send my advisor Tomocomo with you. He and I grew up together. We have never been out of each other's hearts for one day since our childhood. I trust him to watch over you."

Powhatan summoned Tomocomo to the

longhouse. "I want you to sail to London with my daughter Pocahontas and her family," Powhatan said.

Tomocomo looked at his old friend. "I do not want to go to London in this lifetime. Besides, I am too old."

"I cannot go myself," Powhatan said. "My enemies will rise up. The Confederacy needs me here. You must go for me."

Tomocomo, his face and body painted in bright colors, remained silent for a long time.

"I will not order you to go," Powhatan said.

"But I will go for you," Tomocomo finally agreed.

Powhatan gave one of his rare smiles. "Thank you. I want you to do some special favors for me. Ask about Captain John Smith. Is he dead or alive? Don't trust the English too much. I believe they will lie to you. Try to see Captain Smith with your own eyes. See him alive, or find his burial place.

"Also, I want you to count every English person you see. I want to know how many of them are there. That will give me an idea of how many the English king can spare to come here."

Tomocomo took only his Indian clothes of animal skins and a luxurious raccoon coat on the ship.

Pocahontas took her baby's Indian crib board and all her English clothes. Her half sister Matachanna came along to help care for Thomas.

Three more Powhatan women and four men accompanied Pocahontas as helpers and servants. Sir Thomas Dale went along on the voyage, too.

Pocahontas's brothers went to the Jamestown harbor to wave good-bye to their sister.

"Powhatan reminds you to come to see

him as soon as you return. He will wait for word of you every day now," they told her.

"Tell him he will be the first person I go to see. I love you all," Pocahontas said.

She waved from the deck of the sailing ship for as long as she could see her brothers on the shore. Tears came to her eyes long after she could no longer see them.

"I trust in God and the spirit of my ancestors to take care of me and my family," she said to Tomocomo, who was standing beside her.

Out on the water, a strong breeze chilled her and made her shiver. John Rolfe came to get her.

"Come below, my dear, and get your fur coat," he said to Pocahontas. "It's cold on the bay, and it will be even colder when we get out to sea. I had forgotten how cold it was when I came across."

Pocahontas followed his advice. For six

weeks crossing the ocean, the weather stayed calm. But Pocahontas had to wear her fur coat every day, because even on sunny days, the wind blew very cold across the Atlantic Ocean.

She often talked with the ship's captain. He was her old kidnapper, Captain Samuel Argall. She had long ago forgiven him for taking her against her will to Jamestown. He had changed her life completely. But in the end

she had much to thank him for—her husband, her child, her home.

Tomocomo and the other Indians liked to watch the bright trail of light churned up in the water behind the ship at night. Some of the Indians tried on English-style clothes that the English sailors gave them. The Indians were told they would feel more comfortable wearing jackets, breeches, and heavy leather shoes with buckles in London.

Tomocomo absolutely refused to try on a single English shoe or jacket. He didn't speak a word of English. He used a translator to speak with his hosts.

When the ship arrived in Plymouth, England, on June 12, 1616, Tomocomo looked at the crowd of Englishmen on the shore. Many were businessmen who traded with the colonies. English officials wearing uniforms decorated with gold braid came to greet Pocahontas and her party. Tomocomo began to count—and count—and count.

Everyplace he went, from the ship to the inn where the Rolfes and their Indian friends stayed while in London, he kept counting. Finally he held his head in his hands, rubbed his eyes, and stopped.

He would later tell Powhatan that it was impossible to count the English. London was swarming with people. They were as numerous as "the stars in the sky . . . the leaves on trees."

Tomocomo couldn't believe how many people he saw. Powhatan did not have to worry about all of them traveling to the New World. There were not enough ships to take them all.

Pocahontas was enchanted by London. The city was filled with big buildings. There was Westminster Abbey, where the people who governed England met to make laws. They were called members of the House of

Lords and House of Commons. The two houses together were known as Parliament.

The men in Commons were elected to govern the country by people in the cities all around England.

She saw the largest church she could ever imagine—St. Paul's Cathedral. She was told it was the largest cathedral in the world. She could easily believe it.

Remembering the little white sail nailed to the trees to serve as the first church in Jamestown, Pocahontas laughed heartily to herself.

In her wildest dreams she had never imagined that London was such an enormous place. On the streets she saw a few people of other races—small Asian people with dark, slanted eyes and very straight hair like her own, and very dark, tall people from Africa. Jamestown was a tiny little bubble of a place compared to London.

Tomocomo went everyplace with Pocahontas. She noticed how everybody looked at him, because of the animal skins he wore. Barefoot, he held himself erect and walked proudly.

"What an adventure we are having!" she said to Tomocomo.

"I have come here because of your father," he said flatly. "I hope we do not stay a long time."

Pocahontas was taken to a fine stone building

with many steps leading up to the front door and stone columns. There she met the people who headed the Virginia Company and funded Jamestown. All of them dressed the way Sir Thomas Dale did, Pocahontas noticed, with tight breeches and full skirted jackets and buckles on their shoes.

She herself wore her English-style clothes. Except for her dark complexion, no one could tell she was an Indian right away. It took a few minutes for someone to realize she wasn't really English. She spoke English so well that everyone found it quite easy to chat with her.

Some wives of the Virginia Company owners took her to buy material for more dresses for herself. She had stiff white lace collars and cuffs sewn for her to adorn her dark, heavy clothes. She also got a perky little hat to set atop her hair.

One of the wives, who was about Pocahontas's age, confided in her new friend. "I cannot get over my amazement at the deerskin costumes your people wear. Tomocomo especially is a source of wonder with all his animal skins."

Pocahontas smiled. "I will tell you something. He looks normal to me. Sometimes I feel that I'm the one in a costume. I used to wear doeskin clothes myself. As a child, I wore my hair long and loose down my back. And I went barefoot, too. Can you imagine that?"

"No, I can't," said the woman.

"Yes, that is our custom. You must see the world. That's a great education. It teaches you how many different kinds of people there are and what is really important about them."

One of the men from the Virginia Company came to the inn to see Pocahontas and John Rolfe and give them great news. "Your old friend Captain John Smith lives near London. I asked a favor of him, because I want to present you at court. He wrote to Queen Anne, the wife of King James I, and asked her to receive you. The queen has written back that you'll be welcome. Captain Smith told her about how you helped the English survive in Jamestown. Without you, everyone would have died there. The queen cannot wait to meet you."

"Captain Smith!" Pocahontas cried out. "I thought he was dead! He never came back to Jamestown. They told us he was dead."

"No, he is alive. He is helping settle the colonies in New England. The royal family of England loves him," said the man from the Virginia Company. "Do you have any message for me to take to him? He wants to know how you are."

Pocahontas thought it over for a moment. "No, nothing."

"Then I will tell him you are very well." He had a second surprise for Pocahontas. "We have hired an artist to paint a portrait of you in honor of this trip. Will you pose for your portrait?"

"Yes," she said. "I will do it."

The artist visited the Rolfes at the inn and painted Pocahontas in a velvet dress and high stiff lace collar that rose up behind her neck. And she decided to wear the perky little hat her friend had given her. The painting aptly showed her strong nose and large, wide mouth with lips shaped like a Cupid's bow. Her eyes, very dark and penetrating, held a steady, intelligent gaze.

The day came when Pocahontas and John Rolfe went to the king's palace in the heart of London. She curtsied, as she had been coached to do. The king and queen watched

Pocahontas closely for any suggestion of her "savage" or "heathen" background. But she spoke English very well, she moved gracefully, and she mentioned how much she had loved going to church in London.

She acted just like an English lady with excellent manners. Some people thought she even outshone the queen with her charm. Pocahontas was extremely dignified and attentive.

People asked about her childhood. She told lively stories about her life as a Powhatan princess who had been free to wander where she pleased. She told about the temple where the dead *werowances* were kept as mummies, and where her father would be buried, too. She spoke of the long rivers and vast forests she had left behind.

"You must know that England is actually quite small," the queen said.

"Yes, but there are more amazing things in

one mile of London than in all of the Powhatan Confederacy," Pocahontas said. "London is the greatest city one can ever imagine."

"You are very kind, my dear," Queen Anne said.

The king and queen and all their courtiers smiled and nodded at one another. They loved Pocahontas's easy manner. She was a very natural person. They invited her to court every day for two weeks. They sponsored a theatrical performance written especially for her by a leading dramatist of the day, Ben Jonson.

Pocahontas had a constant stream of eminent British visitors, among them artists, writers, political leaders of the country, and noblemen, at her inn. They adored the charming princess, and she in turn loved their attention.

An Old Friend

As THE time went on, Pocahontas began to sneeze. It was drafty in the palace and chilly in the inn where she stayed. Her forehead felt hot and flushed. Outside it was always cold. Usually it was raining. Her skin became wet with fever.

One day she said to John, "I just don't have the strength to go to court today. Let me sleep."

She stopped going to court and stayed at the inn with her husband and son. John was alarmed and called a doctor.

The doctor said she had a cold, and she ought to be very careful for a few days. She

159

drank bowls of steaming tea for breakfast and hot chicken broth for lunch. She slept most of the day and night.

Three Indians who had accompanied her to England died of respiratory illnesses.

The men who ran the Virginia Company discussed Pocahontas's health with her husband. She wasn't getting better. Not only did she sneeze, but when she coughed, her chest was full of phlegm. The doctor put a hand on her chest and felt a bubbling sensation.

He turned to her husband. "This is serious. This is pneumonia."

"What will we do?" John Rolfe asked.

"There's a fine inn at Brentford," the doctor said. "The weather is much drier there than in London. She must go to Brentford immediately."

They went there by horse-drawn carriage. Pocahontas seemed to get a little better. Her brow wasn't so hot, and she sat out in the sunlight during the day. But she complained of dizziness and weakness. The bubbling in her chest didn't go away.

One morning, the innkeeper came to the room to announce that the Rolfes had a guest.

"Who is it?" John Rolfe asked.

"His name is Captain John Smith," the innkeeper said. "I will bring tea for all of you."

"Captain Smith? No, don't bring tea just yet," said Pocahontas.

Captain Smith appeared at the door and stared at Pocahontas. She stood up, extended her hand in the manner of an English lady, and opened her mouth. But no sound came out. She looked away from him and ran out of the sitting room of her suite and disappeared into her bedroom.

She stared out the window of the room and looked at the clipped green grass of the innkeeper's lawn. She was far away from the

161

wild forests of her native land. She put her hand on her head. It was not as hot as usual.

She knew that her rapidly beating heart had nothing to do with her sickness. She was terribly excited to see Captain Smith again, and she was angry that he had not sent a single word to her in all these years.

She went back to the sitting room. Her husband and Captain Smith were talking. They were reminiscing about their experiences in Jamestown—the hard winters, the scanty food.

John Rolfe had never met Powhatan. Captain Smith was telling Rolfe about the majestic appearance of the great leader surrounded by his warriors in the longhouse.

Captain Smith looked much the same as usual, with his whiskers and wide smile. The creases at the sides of his eyes had deepened, so that even in the shaded room, he seemed to be squinting into the sun. There were deep furrows across his forehead.

But he still had a snappy, bright look in his eyes. This was indeed the dashing man who had inspired her to help his people.

"I cannot believe I am sitting in this room with you," she said. "I was told by everyone in Jamestown that you were dead."

"They told you that to make you believe I was gone and would never come back. They didn't like me very well. I worked them so hard. They thought they would be better off

without me. They were wrong, of course," Captain Smith said.

"Why did you never send word to me?" she said.

"I don't think anyone would have given you a message from me," he answered. "They wanted you to think I was dead."

"You should have tried," she said softly. She tossed her head and raised her little chin. "My father didn't believe you were really dead. He asked us to find out for sure. He felt people would still lie to us, and here you are. You have saved me the trouble of searching."

"I'm thrilled to see you. This is such a happy moment for me. It brings back my best memories," he said.

Pocahontas nodded. "Thank you for coming, Father."

"Why do you call me Father?" asked John Smith.

"You did promise Powhatan what was yours should be his, and the like to you, you called him Father being in his land a stranger, and by the same reason so must I do," she said.

"I'm sorry that I'm not feeling well enough to spend more time with you now," Pocahontas continued. "I have to go to bed and rest, or I may never see Jamestown again myself."

She left Smith and her husband in the sitting room and went into the bedroom. There she lay down on the soft English bed and held her baby Thomas close to her.

They never met again. Pocahontas was busy with her family and her health. Smith would later write in his book *A General Historie of Virginia, New England, and the Summer Isles* that he felt uneasy being called "Father" by Pocahontas, because he was just a commoner, and she was the daughter of a king.

The End of an Era

POCAHONTAS DIDN'T complain, but her fever and chills continued for weeks. John Rolfe became so alarmed that he decided to take her back to their house on the James River. She didn't want to go. John asked the doctor for permission to move his wife and take the long ocean voyage. The doctor agreed. "Perhaps you ought to try it."

Pocahontas smiled at John and decided to go along with his decision. "Don't worry. I'll be all right. Make the arrangements."

John asked the men from the Virginia Company to arrange for his family to go back on the next ship. Captain Samuel Argall was in charge of this voyage, too. His ship was supposed to leave in February 1617, but the winds blew so fiercely over the water that the trip was postponed.

In March, the weather became milder. Then Pocahontas, John, and Thomas boarded the ship in London.

But Pocahontas had not improved. She was thin and frail, and she couldn't walk. John Rolfe carried her onto the boat.

Many people from the Virginia Company went to her cabin to say good-bye. One young wife who had become Pocahontas's friend and had laughed with her about the difference between English and Indian clothing brought Pocahontas a necklace of shiny black beads.

"They're beautiful," Pocahontas said in a whispery voice. "I'll always treasure them."

"Please come back when you're feeling better. I'll be waiting," the young wife said. "See, I am wearing a strand of beads just like yours. We are sisters now."

Pocahontas smiled and squeezed her friend's hand. Then she fell asleep. As the ship sailed down the Thames River, Pocahontas kept dozing, waking up, and gasping for breath.

Her forehead was very hot. Her eyes were feverish and glassy.

Captain Argall came down to see her. He paced the floor for a while, then sent for the ship's doctor.

He immediately noticed how much trouble she had breathing. "She cannot make the trip. She must go ashore."

"Will she be all right?" John Rolfe asked.

"I don't know," the doctor said. "She looks in very poor condition right now."

The ship was passing the town of Gravesend on the shore of the Thames. Captain Argall headed directly for the town. John Rolfe carried Pocahontas in his arms to an inn. A local doctor came to examine her.

Soon he shook his head no at John and took him aside.

"I'm very sorry. There's nothing I can do. I don't think she'll last the night."

John Rolfe began to cry. Tears streamed down his cheeks. He begged the doctor to save his wife. He hugged his son and sat beside Pocahontas.

Seeing her husband so sad, she held his hand. "Everyone must die one day. Take comfort from Thomas. He's a treasure and a joy."

She closed her eyes to sleep again. This time she didn't wake up.

One of John Rolfe's younger brothers, Henry, came to Gravesend and helped with the funeral arrangements. John himself was too upset to make plans for the funeral.

It was a small, quiet Christian service in St. George's Parish Church. Afterward, Pocahontas was buried near the church. Tomocomo, who was there, sang an Indian chant after the English left the graveside. Tears wet his cheeks.

After the funeral, John Rolfe decided to leave his son with a friend in London, saying, "I can't raise Thomas without Pocahontas. I don't know how I'll survive without her myself. Please take good care of him and educate him here. He can come to live with me when he's old enough to survive the hard life in the wilderness and on the farm."

After a little while, Thomas went to live with John's brother Henry and his wife in England. And Rolfe sailed back to the New World alone.

He had the painful task of telling Powhatan that Pocahontas had died in England. Powhatan asked about her illness and her burial.

"I never dreamed that I would outlive my beloved daughter," Powhatan said.

He went into his private place to think about fate. When he came out, he gathered his nobles around him. "I am old. I am passing the leadership of the Powhatan Confederacy to my brother Opitchapan. I am going to live with the Potomacs in their quiet, peaceful village."

From then on, Powhatan kept mostly to himself. But people went to visit him. They still asked for his advice.

The next year, in 1618, Powhatan died. His body was given its place of honor among the *werowances*.

In England, Captain John Smith heard

about Pocahontas's death. In *A General Historie* he eventually wrote, "Poor little maid. I sorrowed much for her thus early death and even now cannot think of it without grief, for I felt toward her as if she were mine own daughter."

After Powhatan died, another of his brothers, Opechancanough, began asserting himself as a leader of the Powhatans along with his brother, Opitchapan.

Opechancanough was a warrior by instinct. He was the one who had originally brought Captain John Smith and his compass to Powhatan.

Opitchapan was a milder, quieter man. Together they acted as the leaders of the Powhatan Confederacy.

For four years, they lived in a state of uneasy truce with the English. All the while Opechancanough wanted to fight with the

English and to try to drive them away. Opitchapan kept urging his brother to stay calm—to live and let live.

But in 1622, Opechancanough couldn't stand it anymore. He wanted to get rid of the English at any cost. So he organized a war party to take the English by surprise. In the battle, which ended the Peace of Pocahontas, many colonists were killed.

John Rolfe, too, died at around this time on his farm.

His son Thomas was seven years old then and growing up happily in England. His uncle and aunt, who were raising him, kept telling him everything they knew about his parents, John Rolfe and Pocahontas. Thomas was proud of them both.

When Thomas was twenty years old, he made a decision. "I'm old enough now. I'm going to Jamestown."

Of course, he didn't arrive there empty-handed to begin as a poor, struggling pioneer. Powhatan had willed his grandson Thomas thousands of acres of land as well as Varina, the farm on the James River which Powhatan had given to the Rolfes as a wedding present. Thomas arrived in Jamestown at a time when tensions ran high between the Indians and the English. They didn't socialize or visit with each other anymore.

But Thomas was mindful of his heritage as an Englishman and an Indian. He visited his Indian relatives all the time, while he lived as a farmer among the English.

He married an Englishwoman named Jane Poythress. They raised their children in the colony.

Throughout centuries to come, the name Rolfe was always honored in the area, which became part of the state of Virginia. Through marriages, the Rolfe family became related to many other Virginians. Their heritage made them among the most respected people in the state.

Three centuries and seventy-three years later, in 1995, a famous popular singer named Wayne Newton in the United States of America claimed that he was descended from Pocahontas. He wanted to honor her memory with memorial tributes in Virginia.

A statue had been placed in the graveyard at Gravesend in England to honor Pocahontas. She had been buried far from home, among strangers. She had always remained a mysterious legend to the people of Gravesend. In the colonies, however, she became famous. Eventually she commanded respect as one of the most amazing figures in American history.

Indians would come to regret that

Pocahontas had helped the English to survive, because their endurance spelled the end of Indian rule in North America. But Pocahontas had wanted everyone to live together in peace with respect for one another's cultures and spirits. The goals of Pocahontas still inspire people today.